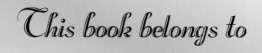

This book belongs to

_____

A Read-Aloud Storybook

Adapted by Lisa Ann Marsoli
Illustrated by the Disney Storybook Artists
Designed by Disney's Global Design Group

Random House 🏠 New York

Copyright © 2004 Disney Enterprises, Inc. All rights reserved under International and
Pan-American Copyright Conventions. Published in the United States by Random House Children's Books, a division of
Random House, Inc., New York, and simultaneously in Canada by Random House of Canada Limited, Toronto, in conjunction
with Disney Enterprises, Inc. RANDOM HOUSE and colophon are registered trademarks of Random House, Inc.
Library of Congress Control Number: 2003113717 ISBN: 0-7364-2217-X

www.randomhouse.com/kids/disney

Printed in the United States of America

10 9 8 7 6 5 4 3 2 1

WANTED

REWARD
$750 for the capture of ALAMEDA SLIM

A Little Patch of Heaven

This is a tale about the three greatest hero cows in the Wild, Wild West. That's right. We're talking about dairy cows who risked their very lives to save their little farm . . . and, as the tale will tell, the rest of the West, too.

It all started way, way back when outlaws struck fear in the heart of every law-abiding citizen. The worst outlaw of them all was Alameda Slim. The sheriff offered a hefty reward to anybody who managed to bring Slim in.

Despite the terror Slim was spreading across the county, everything seemed just fine at a little farm called Patch of Heaven. Pearl, the farm's owner, adored all the animals—especially her two dairy cows, the proper Mrs. Caloway and young Grace.

Then, one day, Pearl made an announcement: "Everybody, this here is Maggie!" Alameda Slim had stolen all the other cattle on Maggie's ranch, leaving the owner penniless—and Maggie homeless. Pearl had agreed to give her a home.

"Wow!" said one of the piggies. "You're the biggest cow I've ever saw!"

"Whoa! Whoa! Dagnabbit, Buck! Slow down!" shouted the sheriff as he galloped onto Pearl's farm atop his cocky horse.

The sheriff pulled a bank notice from his vest. If Pearl didn't pay the bank $750, she was going to lose the farm! And, unfortunately, she didn't have the money.

"I'm sorry, Pearl," the sheriff said sadly.

"Well, 'sorry' just ain't gonna save my farm," replied Pearl as the sheriff rode off.

But Maggie wasn't ready to lose another home. She convinced Grace and Mrs. Caloway to ask Buck for just a little more time to pay the bank. So the three cows took the bank notice and set out for town to find the sheriff's horse. Little did they know they were setting out on the adventure of their lives!

Bovine Bounty Hunters

The town of Chugwater was a strange and scary place to the cows. They heard loud noises everywhere, and humans were roaming free without fences!

"What do we do?" asked a panicked Grace.

Seeing a star on a door, the cows raced inside, thinking they'd found the sheriff's office. Instead, they found the local saloon! The cows accidentally ended up onstage, putting on the best darn show in the West. But the saloon owner soon kicked the cows out for making such a ruckus.

Outside, Maggie, Mrs. Caloway, and Grace bumped into Buck and the sheriff's dog, Rusty. But Buck was too busy daydreaming of being a hero to help the cows. More than anything, Buck wanted to catch outlaws. What did he care about Patch of Heaven?

"Your farm is history!" he rudely told them, as Rusty sniffed at the bank notice.

Just then, swirling clouds of dust darkened the main street as a shadowed figure rode into town. It was Rico, the bounty hunter! And he had an outlaw strapped to his saddle.

"I don't know how you do it, Rico," the sheriff said. "The only varmint left is that low-down, good-for-nothin' Alameda Slim."

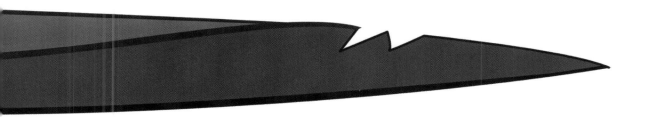

"What's the bounty?" Rico asked.

"Seven hundred and fifty dollars," replied the sheriff. That was the exact amount the cows needed!

"I'm gonna need a fresh horse," Rico announced.

Buck sprang into action and did as many fancy tricks as he could to impress Rico. It worked! Rico saddled up Buck and prepared to hunt down Alameda Slim.

"Hey, Rusty!" Buck cried. "I'm wearing Rico's saddle!" Buck's dreams were coming true!

Meanwhile, Maggie was still thinking about the $750 reward. "Why don't we just capture Alameda Slim and use the reward money to save the farm?" she asked.

"Oh, no!" said Mrs. Caloway.

"C'mon, Caloway!" Maggie said. She butted the older cow playfully, accidentally knocking Mrs. Caloway's hat into the mud!

"Not the hat!" Grace gasped. It was Mrs. Caloway's pride and joy!

Furious, Mrs. Caloway charged toward Maggie.

"What in tarnation . . . ?" the sheriff said. The two dairy cows were having a knock-down, drag-out, Wild West brawl! The sheriff ran over and quickly tied all three cows to the back of the chuck wagon.

"Not exactly what I had in mind, but this'll work," said Maggie.

But Mrs. Caloway was simply annoyed. She was far too dignified to be tied to the back of a chuck wagon!

The chuck wagon set off toward the cattle drive, while Rico and Buck headed out to find Alameda Slim. After a while, the wagon passed a ranch being auctioned off.

"What's going to happen to the cow who lived there?" wondered Grace.

"She'll be okay," Maggie replied sadly.

"How do you know?" asked Grace.

"You're looking at her," Maggie mumbled as a man named Yancy O'Del purchased her former home.

By nightfall, the cows had arrived at a camp where cowboys rested with their herd of cattle. Things seemed quiet enough until—*Thunk! Oof! Whomp!* Alameda Slim's cronies, the no-good Willie brothers, sneaked into the camp and tied up the cowboys!

"Come on, girls! Time to lose these ropes," Maggie said.

Just then, Alameda Slim himself rode in on his buffalo, Junior. Freed from her rope, Maggie charged him!

That was when Alameda Slim reached for his guitar.
He began to yodel. Within seconds, Maggie was in
a trance, and so was Mrs. Caloway. Yodeling was Slim's
secret weapon. It hypnotized cattle!

Luckily, Grace was completely tone-deaf, so Slim's
music had no effect on her. But Grace still had to find a
way to stop Mrs. Caloway and Maggie before
they danced away with Slim!

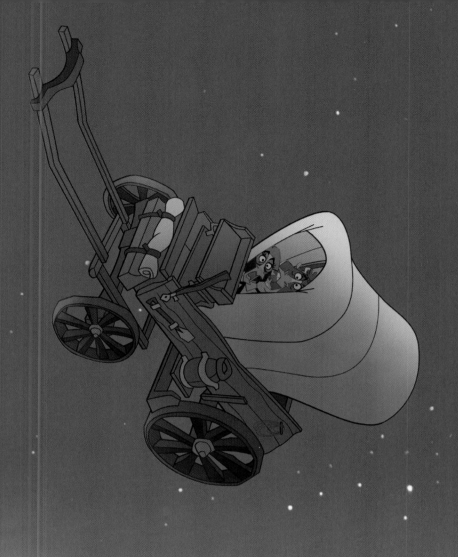

   Still tied to the wagon, Grace ran down the hill as fast as her four legs could carry her. Soon the wagon scooped up Mrs. Caloway and Maggie! Just then, Grace's rope broke, and she found herself flying over the wagon's roof!
   The three cows careened toward the ground . . . and the cattle rustlers!

Down in the canyon, the three cowboys were busy chasing Slim on their horses when suddenly another rider appeared . . . Rico! He was riding Buck. Alameda Slim was surrounded . . . but just for a moment. In a flash, he and the Willies disappeared, along with the entire herd of stolen cattle!

Just then, Maggie, Mrs. Caloway, and Grace burst onto the scene—and crashed into Buck and Rico!

As Rico went to join the cowboys, Buck began to show his fancy hero moves to the cows.

"Give the sheriff back his horse," Rico said as he watched Buck's antics. "This one's too skittish around cows."

Buck was shocked when Rico replaced him. But if he couldn't be a hero with Rico, Buck decided to be a hero on his own!

Meanwhile, Slim and the Willies were hiding out in an abandoned mine with the stolen herd of cattle. When Slim changed his clothes, it became clear that he was none other than Yancy O'Del! It was all part of Slim's plan. He stole cattle, forcing ranchers to go broke and sell their land. Then he went to the auctions dressed as Y. O'Del and bought the land for close to nothing!

"Just one more purchase, and the whole dang territory belongs to me!" he said, greedily looking at his map. Then he branded a dollar sign right on top of Patch of Heaven. The auction of Pearl's farm was only two days away.

Nearby,
Mrs. Caloway, Grace,
and Maggie were trying to
follow Slim's trail. Suddenly, a
flash flood swept them all away. Struggling through
the water, Grace and Mrs. Caloway pulled Maggie to safety
on high ground.

"This whole ridiculous plan is just so you can get
revenge on those cattle rustlers!" Mrs. Caloway shouted.

"This whole ridiculous plan is about saving our
farm!" Maggie yelled back.

Grace looked on sadly as the cows decided to split up
once the storm was over.

The next morning, the cows met a jackrabbit named Lucky Jack. While Jack prepared breakfast for the cows, he explained that he had lived in Echo Mine—until some outlaw had taken it over.

"Wait—there he is!" Lucky Jack shouted, pointing to a reward poster . . . of Alameda Slim! Now the cows knew where Slim was hiding. Maggie and Mrs. Caloway agreed to work together long enough to capture Slim. Then Maggie would leave Patch of Heaven forever.

Lucky Jack and the cows made
their way toward the mine entrance. Buck
was already there, but he couldn't get inside.
Slim's buffalo, Junior, blocked the way.

"The only critters that get by me are cows," Junior
insisted. "Cows only!"

While Buck watched in disbelief, the three cows
walked right past Junior, carrying Lucky Jack with them.

The cows and Lucky Jack were closing in on Alameda Slim. Now all they needed was a plan. And Maggie had one.

"You two get Slim's attention while I sneak up behind him," she told the other cows. "I'll knock him into the cart. Then we rope him up and wheel him to justice!"

But before they put their plan into action, Grace pulled off part of Lucky Jack's cottony tail to plug the ears of Maggie and Mrs. Caloway. She didn't want Slim's yodeling to hypnotize them again!

So Long, Slim!

Inside the mine, Slim quickly spotted the dairy cows. Smiling greedily, he began to yodel. Mrs. Caloway and Grace pretended to be hypnotized and trotted toward him. But before Slim knew what was happening, the cows had shoved him into a mine cart. Then Lucky Jack conked Slim on the head, and away they all raced!

Buck had managed to sneak past Junior and was galloping away from the angry buffalo. Suddenly—*crash!* Buck ended up in the cart with Slim!

"I got Slim!" he cried in shock. "Rico's gonna be so proud of me!"

Soon Buck and Slim barreled into an elevator and rocketed skyward! The cows barely missed catching them—and so did Junior, who was accidentally knocked down the elevator shaft.

"Sorry," said Grace politely.

When Buck and Slim
reached the top of the elevator
shaft, they flew out of the mine
and raced past Rico. *Sccrreeeech!*
Buck stopped the cart. Then he
turned it around and presented
Slim to his hero, Rico.

Buck was one proud horse!

Suddenly, Maggie, Grace, and Mrs. Caloway raced past and snatched Slim away. Rico quickly leaped onto Buck, and together they started chasing the cows to get Slim back. Even Junior joined the chase after he made his way out of the elevator shaft!

The cows rounded a bend in the tunnel . . . and ran right into the Willies. Slim's silly sidekicks jumped onto the cows' cart and pulled the brake lever, showering sparks onto some barrels of gunpowder and dynamite.

Kaboom! Mrs. Caloway, Grace, Maggie, Jack, and Slim went flying out of the tunnel and landed on the railroad tracks outside the mine.

"We made it!" cried Maggie. But the cows' happiness quickly turned to terror. A train was coming toward them at full speed!

Crash! As the smoke cleared, Slim burst out from beneath the cart.

"Dagnabbit! I guess I gotta do everything around here myself," he said, grabbing the three cows and handing them over to the Willies. Then he turned to Rico and tossed him a wad of cash. Rico was Slim's partner!

Buck couldn't believe it! His hero was an outlaw!

"Now if you'll all pardon me," Alameda Slim continued, "there's a little Patch of Heaven on the auction block this morning."

Slim changed into his Yancy O'Del outfit and raced off on Junior. As Rico climbed onto his back, Buck suddenly realized the truth. The bravest, noblest heroes he knew had been right in front of him all along—the dairy cows.

"Make a break for it, ladies!" Buck shouted. He began bucking wildly. Pearl's girls helped Buck finish off Rico and the Willies.

When the dust had settled, Maggie knew that their hope of saving the farm was gone.

"Alameda Slim's already flown the coop," she said.

But Mrs. Caloway wasn't about to give up. "We caught Slim once, and we shall do it again!" she proclaimed. "Who's with me?"

Everyone was! The cows unhooked the engine and climbed aboard. Lucky Jack and Buck ran alongside. The only chance they had of getting Slim and the reward money was to drive the train to Patch of Heaven.

Just as Slim was about to sign the deed that would make Patch of Heaven his, the train arrived!

The three cows wasted no time charging Slim . . . and they were soon joined by the rest of the farm animals. They butted, kicked, conked, pecked, and tickled Slim silly. Finally, Maggie and Grace booted him up to the train's smokestack. A blast from the steam whistle— courtesy of Mrs. Caloway—blew the Yancy O'Del disguise clear off Slim.

"It's Alameda Slim! You're under arrest," said the sheriff. He threw a lasso around the outlaw as the cows watched triumphantly. They had fought the baddest outlaw in the West—and won.

"Pearl," said the sheriff, "your cows can't do much with Slim's reward money. Think you can find some use for it?"

"Whoo-ee!" cried Pearl. "My farm is saved!"

But where was Maggie? Had she kept her promise to leave as soon as Slim was caught? No way! She was just down by the gate, finding a snack.

The next day the whole gang at Patch of Heaven posed together for a picture to be in the newspaper— and Maggie was right there with them! The three cows were famous—but more important, they were all home.